THE MEL NOEL STORY

THE INSIDE STORY OF THE
U.S. AIR FORCE SECRECY ON U.F.O.'S

Mel Noel
Alfred Steber

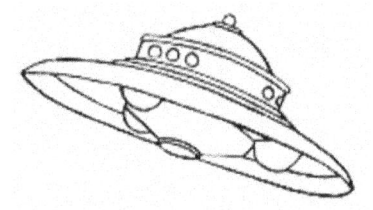

SAUCERIAN PUBLISHER
Original Sources in Ufology

ISBN: 978-1-955087-57-5

9 781955 087575

2023, Saucerian Publisher

On days of good visibility, the squadron flew from Salt Lake City to Boise, Idaho, and back. Machine guns were replaced with three-millimeter cameras which shot 1,100 frames a minute. The cameras were locked into the radar gunsights. When the red light came on, you pressed the button. There was no sophisticated radar lock-on at that time. They squadron had a 90-day tour with extra duty and extra pay. "On the 19th day we saw the UFOs. They were like the bumblebee which, by all laws of aerodynamics, cannot fly. What we saw stopped still, moved straight up and down, then overtook us."

PROLOGUE TO THE EDITION

The pursuit to understand the universe has given birth to various studies, with one of the most fascinating being Ufology, the study of Unidentified Flying Objects (UFOs). Throughout history, numerous individuals have reported sightings of UFOs, among which some are famously controversial and debatable. One such narrative is the Mel Noel (Mel Noel' is a pseudonym for Guy Kirkwood) flying saucer experience, which, despite its contentious nature, continues to captivate UFO enthusiasts and skeptics alike. This prologue will attempt to present Mel Noel's encounter, the subsequent reactions and investigations, and its impact on the broader field of Ufology.

Mel Noel's Encounter:
Mel Noel, a radio broadcaster and experienced pilot, reported his first UFO encounter during a flight to Los Angeles in 1965. According to his account, Noel and his co-pilot observed a "large, metallic, saucer-shaped object" that was approximately 100 feet in diameter, which trailed their aircraft before disappearing. Remarkably, he claimed to have seen the occupants of the saucer, describing them as humanoid, with large heads and eyes. Noel's account bears striking similarities to many others reported during the mid-20th century, contributing to a broader narrative of potential extraterrestrial activity.

The Reaction and Investigations:
Following Noel's report, his encounter was scrutinized by various researchers, enthusiasts, and skeptics. Like many UFO sightings, the narrative was met with a mix of acceptance, intrigue, and skepticism. Some people lauded Noel for sharing his story, while others questioned his credibility, attributing his sighting to natural phenomena, or even discrediting it as a potential publicity stunt.

The U.S. Air Force's Project Blue Book, tasked with investigating UFO sightings between 1952 and 1969, did not officially comment on Noel's case. However, independent UFO researchers and enthusiasts have poured over Noel's account in an attempt to find corroborating evidence or plausible explanations. His report was included in several UFO chronologies, bolstering the narrative of potential extraterrestrial visitation.

Impact on Ufology:
The Mel Noel flying saucer experience had a considerable impact on Ufology. As an experienced pilot and a public figure, Noel's sighting added a significant voice to the growing discourse on UFOs. His account also instigated renewed interest in investigating UFO sightings, contributing to the expansion of the field of Ufology during the 1960s.

While the veracity of Noel's account remains disputed, it highlighted the broader societal fascination with extraterrestrial life and potential visitation. His sighting, like many others, has helped foster a global dialogue on the existence of extraterrestrial life, pushing the boundaries of scientific exploration and prompting humanity to reconsider its place in the universe.

Finally, Mel Noel's flying saucer experience serves as a fascinating case study in the field of Ufology. The ambiguous nature of such encounters, as highlighted by Noel's experience, underscores the complexity of investigating and understanding potential UFO sightings. Despite the skepticism surrounding such accounts, they have undeniably played a significant role in shaping public discourse about extraterrestrial life and the mysteries of our universe. Whether or not Noel's encounter was with an actual extraterrestrial craft, it remains a captivating piece of the broader narrative of human exploration of the unknown.

This book is a facsimile reproduction of the original: ***THE MEL NOEL STORY. THE INSIDE STORY OF THE U.S. AIR FORCE SECRECY ON U.F.O.'S*** published in 1967. **IMPORTANT,even though we have attempted to maintain the integrity of the original work, the present facsimile reproduction may have missing letters and blurred pages, poor pictures due to the age of the original scanned copy.** This magazine has been formatted from its original version for publication. This is a rare and hard-to-find title, and it is almost impossible to get a copy. An essential reference for any serious ufologist. Great, but unpretentious, this issue is an extraordinarily rare symbol of what was going on in those early years of the modern UFO phenomena.

INTRODUCTION

A brief introduction for our speaker. I think one of the nicest things that has come out was in George Van Tassell's Proceedings Magazine. Of all the speakers that were present and on the platform at George Van Tassell's Convention last October when George came to write up the report of that Convention, there was just one of those speakers he wrote about and gave three pages of this magazine to that one. This gentleman is our speaker tonight.

I wasn't able to attend that Convention out at Giant Rock last October, so I didn't know anything about the speakers they had, but I heard about Mel Noel from all directions. Everyone who had been out there was very much impressed. He had a message, he had a different message and a vital one, a true one and of a level that we all have to look to and respect to a great extent.

The information that we sent out in our bulletin that most of you received in the mail a week or so ago gives the information about Mr. Noel. But for those who did not receive such bulletins, I'll give it very briefly.

Up to twelve years ago, Mr. Noel was a Lieutenant in the United States Air Force, flying a jet plane, and he had experiences that, I suppose, no other Officer, Air Force Officer who has possibly had the same experiences, has had the courage to come out and face the persecution and the adverse as well as good publicity because of telling of his experience. However, he wasn't allowed to tell such for at least ten years after he left the Air Force. So as soon as he was able to, he began telling of the facts of the experience that he had.

We are very proud to have and very happy to have Mr. Mel Noel as our speaker tonight. We are one of the very few privileged audiences to hear him.

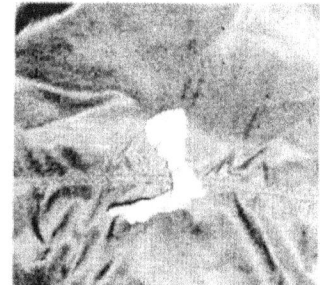

Purported piece of a UFO which has denied all analysis.

Mel Noel with just some of his many auto racing trophies.

P U B L I C   L E C T U R E

by

MR. MEL NOEL

Mr. Yates, Mr. Gahlbeck. Thank you. I'd like to say, give an acknowledgement here to Gabriel Green especially since he is here. I wouldn't be here if it were not for him. He is the one who talked me into talking about it. It was sort of the end of the road for a frustrated civie as to what to do with what happened.

It would seem that we all and all those who are not here, are involved in a time, a time in the life of a planet, a universe or whatever. That instead of reading about history, instead of yesterday or instead of wondering what's going to happen tomorrow, all we have to do is open our eyes cause its happening now. Its going on around us, its all over the world, and yet we wonder how long the eyes have been closed, because its been happening. Its not just starting.

Miss Forrester answered an oft asked question as to why you waited so long in doing anything about this. I want to clarify a couple of points though Roberta, that it isn't exactly quite that way.

As far as relating, discussing our experiences, it is a security matter. I don't know if you understand the interpretation of security or not by the Government of the United States, but their interpretation is, 'this is information or knowledge, tangible or otherwise, which is withheld from the public's knowledge for the public's safety.' Many people will agree with this.

I find, at least I have come to believe, that this is a form of mental rigor mortis, and its prevalent; its all over. People are too prone to accept, and it is very easy to be led or to be gullible, shall we say, because of our desires or because of what we are indoctrinated into. I have been affected by this as much as any one else. Not so much now, but some years ago.

It is very difficult to be objective about something which is unknown. Realism is something that's standing in front of you. Its a desk, its a book, its a window, I can touch it, I can see it; things that relate to our common senses. We can begin to comprehend and understand those things.

The entire thing is a mystery. Many people say, "Gee, your an authority on it." Answer this, answer that. I know very little. Its true I may know much more than a lot of other people, but relative to the entire situation, I still know very little.

Just like a mystery, a mystery is like a mathematical equation. You have so many givens, and you have so many unknowns. Now we're collecting the givens, and the more givens, the more theories we can evolve and we can develop. And from this which is all of physics, all of physics is theory, what somebody imagined, and it leads us to something until we have fact. Sometimes we are not sure of fact even when we see it. We're not used to it. Our environment has not been such.

I mentioned before, its difficult to be objective about something, and I want you to be honest to yourself when you weigh these things. I want you to understand that part of this was first person. The greater part of it was related to me and related to the other two officers involved. I want you to be objective about it. I want you to look at it by your instinct, shall we say. I find its never wise to pass judgment on anything, at any time as such, unless I am forced to. We all have our moments of truth where we have to make a decision; we make a hundred a day. But on something like this, its so important that you must put the issue in the center and build the case, pro and con along side, each side of it, and keep building that, eventually you will know what the answers are, as long as you keep seeking.

I mentioned before I wouldn't be here if it weren't for Gabe Green. After so many years, its very difficult after the warnings from security, the statements and the exercising to other individuals who were your friends, the violation of security. I think you'll understand why, as I relate this to you.

Let's go back now. This happened in 1953 and in the earlier part of 1954. In 1953 we had just come out of the Korean War. None of us were involved in the Korean War, it ended while we were in flight school. We were assigned to a reserve squadron in the western part of the United States, we were what we might best call 'line pilots'. You have so many duties to perform, you had to fly so many hours a year, so much of it was gunnery, so much was cross country, so much instrument time and aerobatics and such.

We hadn't been with the squadron very long when we were taken apart, three of us, myself, a Lt.   , a Lt.   , and we were notified that we were being released from our duties as line pilots. We were being placed on operation, called 'operation units.' They told us at the time it was a security matter, and they then took us into the briefing of it. We don't to this day know why we were selected for it. I don't know whether they just took the roster and threw darts at it on the wall or whether they picked it for other reasons, but we had been picked.

They began by explaining the nature of the operation as to the fact that it concerned the UFO, the flying saucers as is better known. They explained to us that if and when anything happened concerning them, as far as relating it, discussing it with friends, relatives, even fellow-officers, the statement to us was, don't even talk to yourself about it. You put it down on the report and take it out of your head and that's where it ends.

They briefed us with several hours of motion picture films that were taken, had been taken by government military aircraft. They showed us many hundreds of still photographs, some were taken by the government, many of which I understand were confiscated from civilizns. We were instructed for a number of hours on specific aerial maneuvers, weave patterns, formation flying, the operation of the cameras. We were instructed, we were notified that all the armament, the weapon system, the fire system had been removed from the aircraft.

The aircraft were what was known as F 86A Sabre Jets. Their standard system, standard firing system is 6 - 50 caliber machine guns. These had been all removed and replaced with cameras, gun cameras. Some of these cameras we were informed, contained standard film. The others contained infra-red film. If you're not familiar with infra-red film, infra-red film will take a picture of something that you cannot see. In other words, you can be vectored into an area on a target that you cannot see by radar and take pictures of objects. You won't see them then, they only come out after the film is developed.

After all the briefing, we discussed it briefly. We had been turned over to a Colonel who was not with the squadron. He was assigned to the operation out of Washington, D.C. We were to respond only to him, have nothing to do any longer with the squadron. He was our flight leader through our entire experience and later on became a very close friend. At the time however, he was as military as you can find somebody. Everything was strict order. He wanted to discuss nothing else, personal, social or topics of the time in any other way shape or form. It was all business.

The three of us,   · and I discussed, prior to the experiences, our common opinion was, that nothing was going to happen. We were aware of the position of the Air Force on it - that there were many reports, that the Air Force made claim to have investigated these things, and we figured that we were in essence the dumb dumbs, that we were going through the paces to live up to these statements. In other words, we were to investigate these things. This was it! But we really didn't expect to see anything, let alone hear anything.

The first few missions were, we might say, the orientation runs. We were closing up our formation flying under different conditions. We were operating at approximately 38,000 ft. altitude, 6 or 7 miles above the surface of the earth, and we were operating over the Rocky Mountains of Idaho, Utah and on up north. The first week produced the first sighting. I mentioned before we had been instructed in formation flying. If you can imagine, we flew in what is called a diamond formation.

If you can picture a baseball diamond. Second base is the flight leader. Third base is left wing man. First base is the right wing man. Home plate is called slot position. I drew the slot position; I didn't like it, but that's what I got. The operation was to maintain this formation, this diamond formation. Upon a sighting the formation was closed in, 60 ft. was from wing tip to wing tip. We were drilled until this became measurable almost to the inch. As soon as a sighting was made, a visual contact, there was an order change; we broke into a weave pattern. Now the weave pattern operated this way. As soon as the formation broke, second base and third base broke starboard, that means broke right, and home plate and first base broke left onto the target. If the target were dead ahead, it was projectory all ahead.

If it were left, it would be home base and first base that would have first projectory. It it were on the right, third base and second base would have first projectory.

As it happened, the sightings were all to our left, and the first one to see them was   '. He always saw them first; I don't know why. It wasn't what he said, but how he said it I think, that got to all of us real quick. His statement was, "Bogies, nine o'clock level." Bogey is just Air Force slang. It just means foreign aircraft, something you don't know what it is, something that don't belong to us, and we were convinced of that. There were 16 of them, and they were operating in a verticle V formation. They were strung out seven and nine, seven aloft and nine going aft.

They were operating at approximately the same speed. They maintained right along side of us. We were operating 680 knots. That was surface speed. Military jets, there are two speeds, two air speeds; you have surface and military speeds. Surface is a cruising speed as it is better known in civilian aircraft, and military is everything that can be put into the boiler, the after burner. You can get up into over 700 miles an hour. We could not obtain mach one or speed of sound in level flight, but we could obtain it in a dive. We very seldom did it because of the vibration incurred, so we were maintaining our surface speed, and they were maintaining at the same speed and the same altitude as we were.

At this speed their appearance was a relatively distinct physical outline with a best described 'aura' surrounding them. I think perhaps the best way of relating this aura is, if you have ever seen a street light or a neon sign in a fog, in the rain, they seem to be very fuzzy, and this is the type of appearance it gives.

The effect upon myself – I was pretty excited! I didn't know what was happening. I had never seen one of these things before, let alone 16 of them. And a thousand questions raced through your mind, and as fast as these questions come, your moving. The weave was called and off we went, and were closing on them, and we were given very distinct closing minimum distances. In other words, you don't get too close. We already knew what had happened to aircraft that had gotten too close, and we didn't want to go through that.

We, to the best of my knowledge, did not get any, very few if any, photographs, pictures, the first time. The reason being was that the cameras had been hooked up with the automatic gunsight system. This automatic gunsight is a little electronic wonder which pins the target, holds the target, goes through a series of electronic manipulations and aims the guns and fires them. This all takes 20 some odd seconds under standard conditions, and it wasn't enough, it wasn't fast enough; it had taken too long. I think the cameras triggered several times, but it was too late. We had to back off on the opposite leg by that time.

If you can picture this weave, we would break when we are in our formation; this is the slot and rightwing man breaking toward left. We are now closing on a target, a common target. We are closing projectory. In other words, if we were to go to target, we would collide ourselves, so as we would reach approximately 100 ft. wingtip to wingtip, the wide man would go low, he would go under and the near man would come over and reverse position, and we would then reverse and come back 90 degrees on our next leg back. In the meantime, the other two men had reversed their leg, and were now heading on target.

The effect or purpose of this, was to have two aircraft on the same target at all times. In other words, confirming evidence, opinion of pilot as well as camera. Whatever was produced, there were two people looking at the same thing at the same time. At the same time when you reversed your leg, you were blind. You couldn't see it, but the other two pilots were covering you at all times. If anything were happening, they would notify you.

Our weave pattern didn't go on very long because they broke their formation into four groups of four. This answered a question. We thought perhaps they were centrally controlled by one unit and they were locked on and controlled, however it was, we didn't know how they were propelled, and they split into four groups of four, and then after a minute or so, they split individually, and they demonstrated some things that by the book can't happen. And its like the bumble bee, he can't fly - that's by the book, but he doesn't know that, so he goes ahead and does it. These things were doing things that you couldn't do in the air according to the book. It was impossible for a human being if there were human beings in them, we didn't know then, to survive the breaking from what we were estimating their top speed at approximately 3,000 miles an hour, to a dead stop, and I mean instantly! Just as fast as when you turn the switch off the lights go off, that's as fast as they stopped, and they accelerated just about as fast. When they turn the juice on, they are going. As they would accelerate, when they would stop, the physical outline was very clear.

They were approximately 150 to 180 ft. in diameter and about 20 or 30 ft. thick at the widest midsection, cross section. One point that we didn't agree on was whether the center section was approximately 30 or 40 ft. in the center of the saucer elevated, raised out when they would stop. It was so difficult; they would operate so fast, and our observation was at times so limited, it was difficult to tell whether the center section was raised all the time or whether it just elevated when they would stop for observation. As they would accelerate, the haze around them, the aura would change color just like the spectrum. In other words, if you were to go over the spectrum, they would advance through those various stages. There was no evidence of sound, we of course being sealed in, we couldn't smell anything; we couldn't feel anything. Other than slight compass malfunction, we did not have any instrument malfunction. All systems operated normally. The compass malfunction is not unusual anyway. You get this in many areas, and we didn't experience any ill and uncomfortable effects ourselves, other than what we would have put in our own minds.

The entire experience lasted about eight minutes and as quickly as they appeared, we didn't see them coming, but as quickly as they appeared, they were gone. I mean when they go, they go. They strung off just like a string of beads, and you could count them out of sight. We were pretty excited about the entire thing! This certainly was something new. We didn't know what to think of it. As far as we knew, we were safe. Everything was going along fine. When we landed, we were reminded of the security. We were given reports; we filled the reports out. Whether we got any films or not, we don't know, they pulled the cans as fast as we landed and we never did see them; we didn't even know where they went.

The security was constantly pointed out to us. It was reminded to us exactly, not what would happen if, but we had an example of this, not during our experience, I shouldn't say this, but it was right around the same time. One of the line pilots, he was not on this assignment, just in his regular line of duties, had seen a few of them. And he decided that he was going to tell more than just a few people about it, so he sold to Fawcett Publications what he saw, and he received $500.00 for his efforts, and within 24 hours after he had signed the contract with them, the article hadn't had a chance to appear of course, within 24 hours after he signed the contract, he was in the Aleutian Islands, he was reassigned. Now at that time, it was commonly known as a suicide assignment, its a one way ticket. Its one you get that you don't come back from. So, of course, this weighed over us. We thought a great deal about talking about this to anybody.

Many, many questions occurred to us. We would discuss these for many hours alone, just the three of us, cause the Colonel wouldn't talk to us about it. We didn't know whether it was just happening to him or what was going on at that point.

We flew a number of missions between the sightings without anything happening, and it was just like any other run. The second time was a few days later, and this time there were only five of them.   spotted them again. In the meantime we had, by our recommendation, they had changed the triggering of the cameras from the automatic to the manual. In other words, the stick buttons, which meant that we could fire or just shoot as many frames as we possibly could at any time, and I'm certain that we obtained a number of photographs this way. I remember now, our calculations of aiming were up to us, up to our eyes rather than by electronic calculations. If given the proper amount of time, the gunsight would have done a much better job, but in case of expediency here, we didn't have enough time, so they had converted it.

The second experience was just like the first, as far as what we were seeing. We didn't know if they were the same ones or not, but there they were, there were just five of them! They moved about, up and down, in verticle oscillation, down this way. When they would turn or change direction, there was no bank, they were unaffected it would seem by the various laws that had been drilled into us for months and months in flight school; the laws of lift and drag, yaw and gravity. The forces of stopping or acceleration didn't seem to affect anything or anybody, that we knew. We felt we were getting used to it, and yet something was going on inside of us that we hadn't begun to understand. It was all very exciting!

When something is exciting, you're only focusing upon what is happening, not on what it means. This was brought home, I think, very seriously on the third sighting. When it was made, there were five again, this was just a couple of days later. When   called, we were looking, and he notified us that they were there, at the time we assumed things, and you shouldn't do that, we assumed the change of position of weave and in close formation, 60 ft. tip to tip, you haven't got much room for mistakes and there was a little jockeying there, because the call never came. He didn't call a change, and after less than a minute, we had a change of radio channel. This was given to us in a code which is called an inverted alphabetical code. If you take WXYZ and invert that numerically, it would be 1-2-3-4. This is the way the codes were changed or the radio channels were changed, through this alphabetical system. We were given the letters - it took me probably 20 to 25 seconds to convert it, convert the letters and figure the numerical values and then to spin it in. And what I did, I didn't know of course, in that short span of time, you're not wondering why you're doing something, you're just doing it, and this is just part of your orientation.

You go through quite a bit of, a moment of truth searching during something like this. You wonder why its happening to you. You wonder what you're doing here, what this is all about. It starts coming to you and you don't have time to think about it. We thought we were getting used to seeing these things. We could live with them! But the experience of the communication was something that we weren't really ready for, and we didn't expect it and couldn't understand what this was all about.

When I hit the channel, there was a voice speaking on it and it was not me; it wasn't either of the group, anyone of the flight, or the other three. And the voice was answering questions as such. Now, at no time did I ask any questions. At no time did any of the other three pilots ask any questions, uttered them verbially, and yet we were hearing something that was coming through, just like we were listening to or talking to each other or to a tower on the ground. It was very clear. The ennunciation, pronunciation, vocabulary was excellent. The rate of speech was very slow. We were told later on by the flight leader, by the Colonel, that he had been asking the questions.

He said, "I did not say any of them." He said, "I was merely thinking them." He said, "They did not answer all of them, just a few." The first statement that had been made, and we had to at this time remember, more or less read in what the question might be, which he later on told us. He said the first question was, "Do you believe in God?" Now, he said, "the reason I asked them this was, if there was somebody there and they did, and if they did, then the odds were with us that they weren't hostile." And the answer, the statement was that we heard was, "We believe in the Almighty Power of the Universe. You must understand that there are over 150 billion universes, and that there are many forms and orders of Gods in each and everyone of them."

I am not relating to you verbatim. After 12 years, I can't remember exactly word for word, but this is very very close to the exact wording of what was said. Something like this doesn't leave you as such. The next statement was referring to the existence of life here, where they came from, what they believed in. They said that, ah, the question had to be - he said the question was - do you - I am trying to think of what excited the question, exactly how the question was worded, because the statement was in effect, - The existence of Noah in the Bible, the authenticity of it as such, they referred to it as an erroneous history book. They said for instance, "Noah's Ark was never a boat. It was an are of time or a period of time, which this man was a Ruler, and he ruled over a civilization, and he said if we went back and investigated the Latin, we would find Noah meant Inca, and the Incas were the last of the Noah civilization."

And they referred to, they made the statement that our scientists had made statements based upon theories that life cannot and therefore does not exist on the other planets in this system, and they said that they were confirming those statements. He said, "Life does not and cannot exist on these other planets; its all inside the planets, its all in the interior, just as the

house of the Lord. This is the house of the Lord we live in, the interior of
the planet, and they stated that life originated here the same way, on the
interior of the planet. And he said that it still exists that way."

The next question must have been as to exactly who are you, where
are you from? Because the statement was, "Our crews are made up of individuals from planets known to you as Venus, Jupiter, Mercury, Mars and Saturn,
and they referred to Saturn as the head Tribunal Planet." In other words, the
leaders of the state met here to discuss the affairs of state. They went into a number of other things that may or may not be important; by discussion
with legal advice, much of this, I can only discuss about 10 per cent of what
took place.

The total effect of the experience on us was when we landed, we
couldn't walk! We were crawling! We were on our hands and knees, and we
weren't ready for it. All we wanted was out, and this is what we told them
then. They gave us sedation; we told them we said, we want out of this, we
don't want any more to do with it, anyway we can get out of it. Whether it
was his efforts or not, we were relieved of the assignment the next day. One
thing that was out of order was that as soon as we landed, he insisted, he
dictated to us and he said, "You do not report the communication." He said,
"Everything else, but do not report the communication." This is unusual. We
didn't care to report anything.

It was a relief to get away from it and back to the regular duties.
The problem was now, how do you live with it? I talked to veterans of combat
and seen some of the psychological effect of first hand combat. I don't know
if any of you here have seen combat. I have not. I hope you haven't from
what I have seen, the effect of it upon others; its a brutal thing. And yet,
some of this is similar to it. You weigh mankind. You weigh your own and you
weigh the thinking of the world, and you say where does this fit, where does
this fit in my thinking, in my way of life? Well, I have no time for it. I
haven't got the answers. I don't know where to go to get the answers, so I'm
going to pass. I'm just going to go ahead just like everybody else. There's
a couple hundred million people living, having, having a good time, and I can
do the same thing, I can do without this, and its not easy to do without it.
Not that you want it, something happened to you. You were involved whether
you wanted it or not, and here you are now, what are you going to do with it?

I discussed it with two people in ten years. My father was one
of them, and after I got through, I spoke to him for several hours, I told
him everything and he said that you didn't have to be in the Air Force for it
to happen. I looked at him and said, "What are you talking about? Have you
been there?" and he said, "Do you remember when you were back in prep school?
He said, I was reading this book, I read this book and I recommended it to you.
I thought it was an excellent work." I said, "That's a long ways away, Dad."
And he said, "What do you mean? Four years isn't long." It was longer than
four years then, it was about ten years, and he said, "I told you to read
'Oahspe' then." And I said, "Oh yea, I remember now." And he said, "You
didn't read it though?" And I said, "No I didn't. I said it didn't pertain
to my interest at the time or my school studies so I never got around to it."
And he said, "You'll find much of what took place and what the statements
were in there".

So I just recently started the book. Its about 900 pages. Its not easy reading, not by my opinion anyway. I'm into it about 30 pages and I'm already finding things. Its in there, much of it. I also understand there's two different editions of this book and that one is not as correct or not correct, and the other one is, but I'm not sure which one is or isn't. This doesn't make it too easy. I hope I don't have to read two of them.

This was just the first part of it, because the real testing was coming into being. For about two months after we were off the assignment, we began to figure that we could live with this thing. The three of us, the other two pilots and I talked about it quite a bit, and we decided that we couldn't help each other very much. The answers weren't here. It was just opinion against opinion. We could only confirm what all of us had seen and heard, so where do you go from here? The Colonel wouldn't talk to us. About two months later he called me up and he said, "Come on over, I want to talk to you." And I said boy maybe this is it, maybe these are the answers.

When I got over there,   and   had already gotten there. The Colonel was very nervous. He was pacing up and down, and he said, "I've got to talk to somebody." He said, "I've got to let you know what's happening." And we just sat there with bated breath as to well let's have it! He said, "I've got to make a decision." He said, "I'm not asking for your help in making the decision; I'll do that myself." He said, "I just want to associate with somebody who can understand," and he said, "I think you fellows are the only ones with whom I can do it."

He said, "I've found the truth," and then he made a statement which I think he was making for his own benefit as well as ours. He said, "I am an Officer in this Government, in this Armed Forces, in the United States Air Force, and I have a duty, a responsibility and an image to maintain," and he said, "The truth doesn't agree with it." He said, "I've got to go one way or the other." He said, "I can't live with both." He said, "I don't know what they do with what's happening, but its not getting out," and he said, "That's all," and it was. He wasn't going to discuss anything else. He said, "I'll see you later," and bid us goodnight.

So what we thought was going to happen, didn't happen at all, except we didn't realize that he had opened the door. We were in for almost about ten months of experiences of his that he related to us concerning these things. And it was several weeks later before he called again. This time he called, he said, "Come on over," and he said, "I'm going to let you in on it." We went over; I got there the other fellows came in.

We sat down and he told us that this wasn't new to him by any means, he had been on this for quite a while. He said, "The communication wasn't the first time. It was the first time anybody else was along when he had communication. He said that he had innumerable experiences with them. He felt that his experience was invaluable as far as the procedures of the Government, of the Air Force now in tracking and pursuing them because of it." And then he started to relate some of the experiences to us.

It seemed by his statements that the experiences were always three or four months old, they hadn't just happened, and most of them varied little except for the time and the place, the weather conditions, the speeds and the shapes of the objects. He explained to us that saucers were incapable of flying from planet to planet. He said, "They can't do this because they operate in the electronic - electrical fields surrounding the planets." He compared this to a current of electricity in a piece of wire. In other words, if you take a piece of wire, and you conduct electrical current through that wire and you can control the speed of that flux, the current through that wire by resistance, - now by inverting that theory, we pass the wire through the field and control the speed by resistance once again. I guess it doesn't work quite that easy, but this is how he compared it. This is how they operate.

"Even though the electrical fields overlap between planets," he said, "they are not strong enough at the outer distances so these saucers are carried by mother ships." He said, "The mother ships were up to ten miles long and they would carry as many as 300 saucers. They had several thousands of crews and he said, they all came from different planets, and he said, they even came from planets outside this galaxy."

He said, "It only took a few minutes to go from here to another planet, because the mother ship was capable of the speed of light at which time it becomes infinity, that there is no time passage as such, as we know it here."

The one experience that he related to us which I think was outstanding was the contact he had with them...when he spoke with the, he saw them, and he related this to us the very next day after it happened. He called me up and he was very excited! He said, "Get over here fast!", and I did. He said, "I've seen them; I drove with them to where the saucer is. I talked with them. I talked with a guy called a Master! He has the most fantastic mind that I ever talked to." And we said, "Well, settle down Pete. Let's hear it."

He said that he had had a cross country the night before, he was flying to Luke Air Force Base, that's out in Phoenix, Arizona. He said that on the way down, it was uneventful, nothing had taken place. He said it this way. "I don't know what you think about dreams." He said, "Now don't get me wrong, I wasn't asleep." He said, "I was wide awake." He said, "I had a daydream or a sequence thing or whatever you want to call it, but I had a little sequence thing in which I imagined or dreamed that after I had gotten landed on the field and went into operations, they told me that they have reserved a staff car for me," (and this is not unusual for a man of his rank), and they told him that they had reserved a motel room for him (and that's not unusual). He said, "that after he got to the motel, the room clerk told him the number of the room, and he said that at 7:30 that night there was a knock on the door and he said that there were two men there at the door that he had never seen before." He said, "That's where it ended, that's as much as I had received as such." He said, "That's all I knew about it."

"Well, he said, that when he got down there and he went into operations, they told him they had reserved a staff car for him." He said, "I passed that off as just a coincidence." And he said, "they told me they reserved a motel room for me." He said, "even though it was the same name of the motel, I passed that off as just a coincidence. There are just so many motels there at that time." He said, "But when I got to the motel and the room number coincided, he said, I started getting upset." He said, "I figure that three out of three was going pretty strong, and he said, I took a hot bath and I tried to settle down; I laid down, I tried to read." And he said,

"After awhile, I couldn't get my eyes off that clock and at 7:30 there was a knock on the door." And he said, "I didn't know whether to go to the door or out the window." He said, "I figured I had been through an awful lot and maybe this is it; this was too much!"

He said, "I knew I was perhaps reading into it and I went to the door. I opened the door, and there were two young fellows standing there about college age. They had suits on and hats, and he said the only unusual thing about them was their eyes." He said, "Their eyes looked as if they could look right through you." And he said, "The one fellow, they addressed him by his name and rank, and they introduced themselves and they said their names were Mike and Dave for all practical purposes." And he said, "The fellow who was speaking, called himself Mike; he extended his hand, and he said, "I extended mine, and I shook hands with him." He said, "The only definition I can use was a feeling that went through me when I did it." He said, "It was love. That's all I know." He said, "I never experienced anything like that before between man and woman in my life. That's just what it was. I put my life in his hands at that moment," he said, "if he would have told me to jump off the Empire State Building, I would have done it and I wouldn't have been hurt." He said, "I didn't know what I was in for, but I no longer feared anything."

He said, "We went outside; we got in a car, a Chevy car. We drove outside of Phoenix. They informed me that they were taking me aboard a saucer, and they were going to allow me an audience with a man they called the Master." And he said, "That they told him that a Master was the highest physical form, that this was the highest form physically in intelligence, and then after that an individual becomes a God-aether." And they said, "That he had performed well in his duties, and this is why he was being allowed this audience." They said, "It would take approximately a half hour so that he could prepare any questions that he wanted to ask." And he said, "He was trying to focus, trying to be objective about it." So he said, "That it was pretty, pretty exciting!".

He said, "They got out, I figured about 18 miles outside the city and they left the main highway and they drove off a little road into the desert. And after awhile, in that area the property of the land was very rolly, very hilly and it was growing dusk, he said, and they turned the headlights on the car, and then they drove off the road." He said, "After awhile they came over a bluff, the car stopped; they hadn't turned the switch off though, or the lights off though, but the lights and the engine stopped and he said he could look out and see the bottom of a valley, so to speak, there." He said, "There was a saucer sitting there on a tripod, on three legs." He said, "It was about 150 ft. in diameter." He said, "It was just sitting there, that's all."

He said, "They got out of the car and when they did, these two fellows took their suits and hats off and their shirts, and they had a one piece jump-type suit on underneath." He said, "This was one piece including the shoes and that they wore a belt, and the belt had a metal disk in it, in the center of it." He said, "They produced one of these metallic disks for him and they told him to hold it between the palms of his hands." He showed to us, like this. And he had the disk, he still had the disk, he showed it to us. And they said, "To hold it in the palms of his hands and hold it to his stomach, and this would guarantee no ill-effects when passing through the force fields as he entered the saucer."

He said, "They walked until they were about 80 ft. from the saucer and stopped and they just stood there." And he said, "I started to talk, and they just looked at me; that was enough to say, just be quiet for now." And he said, "After a moment, there was a sort of a ramp that came down from the saucer and a man came down out of it." And he said, "The fellow stood out there." He said, "Although there was no verbal uttering going on, it was fairly obvious that they were discussing things, that they were talking things over, and they then turned to him and said, its alright, everything is okay, we can go aboard." And he said, "They walked to the ship, he said, the man who had come outside had already gone back in; they all walked in there."

He said, "The entire place glowed like a, in other words, there was no concentration of light as we have it here, we see it in these bulbs. The ceilings, the floors, and the walls, they all glowed equally." He said, "They took me first to the control section, the center of it." He described it to us. He said, "They described it fairly well to him exactly how the thing operates; their speeds, their controls." He said, "They had many control systems that were similar to ours already, their use of television and radar as such. They had these systems also."

He said, "They also told him about scout ships, they were unmanned, they were merely instrument packages; these things were just four to six feet in diameter. They could send these out and control them, radio control them and put them into an area where they would be undetected where a larger craft would be spotted. They said they could send these in and relay information back." In other words, they would send back a telecast just as we would from a telestation and produce it on a screen there in the saucer and they could see it.

He said, "They took him into an outer room then and informed him that it was about time for his audience, and he said he walked into this room, and he said, it was always difficult when you changed rooms to tell whether the lights just went on or they were already on, he said, but it seemed to be always new brilliance and the lights were particularly strong but not uncomfortable." He said, "He sat down on a bench affair on the outside, he said he could tell they were on the outer perimeter because the roof slanted, and he said they sat there for a few minutes."

"After a few minutes, two women came into the room, and he said that by the way you fellows think as well as myself, well, I'm just a red-blooded American boy and he said, they were pretty groovy chicks." And he said, "They were real beautiful women, so he said, you know after all, I'm progressive and he said, I just came into my natural way of thinking!" He said, "They started laughing and giggling and I all of a sudden realized that they knew what I was thinking."

He said, "I was very embarrassed." He said, "I went to get a cigarette and he said, I noticed I hadn't seen anybody smoking or even facilities for such, and they explained that it was just a nasty habit I had here and that I would get rid of it sooner or later. And they asked him if he was thirsty and he said he could have drank the Red Sea dry about then." And he said, "They went out and brought back a glass of what he closely compared to as grape juice; he said it wasn't unusual." He said, "After I said yes, I'm thirsty, all of a sudden I realized maybe they were going to give me a glass of Bardahl, or a glass of lye, and maybe I wasn't ready for this, but he said it wasn't unpleasant at all."

And he said that when they went out of the room to bring him back this glass of whatever it was, he said, the one fellow turned to him and he said, "How old do you think the young ladies are?" "I told him I figured they were about 18-19-20 years old, at the oldest." He said, "Maybe you would be interested to know that the one is 78 years old, and the other one is 146." And he said, "You know, that's the first time I ever thought of making love to a 146 year old woman."

He said the ladies hadn't come back the second time, but two other men came into the room and this Master came in. And he said it was obvious that the Master was a senior person by his dress. He said, "They all wore these one-piece jumpsuit outfits, but he said, they also had these little colored patches on their suits. He said that one of the men explained that this established their degree of intelligence, in other words, the rank of intelligence. He said the Master was introduced to him, was told that this Master was from Venus, and he sat down."

The Master told him, "You may ask me any question you want, but I won't necessarily answer any of them." He said, "Of course I went into high gear again with my questions as to what I felt most important, so I started repeating the questions that we had in our communications, and he said the answers were almost the same." In other words, "Do you believe in God?" "Yes, to the Almighty Power of the Universe." He said, "There are many degrees and forms of Gods and many spiritual aethers, he said, they go on and on and on." And he said, "But as it is related in that fine little history book called the Bible that you have, he said, "As God is, man may become." He said, "That this is so, you will become. We all go through the same."

And he said that he asked him what was happening, what was taking place, why they were coming, what was going to be taking place in the future. And he said that, "We think of it here that they are responsible for the planet as long as it has been here." He said, "They are assigned positions of responsibility in which they have control or are responsible for so many hundreds of millions of spirits." He said, "Reincarnation was a problem because it was difficult to send so many people back. He explained that they had assumed certain important responsibilities as to the conditions of this planet, and he said that things weren't too good here." Heck, we already knew that! And he said that, "This was more as a clearing house and that they sent their problem makers over here for awhile." I guess we got them all!

He predicted a number of things. He made statements pertaining to the future. Now at this time, this was in 1954, these predictions were interesting, fascinating to hear, but relatively, personally, they weren't that important. He made certain remarks concerning California in 1967, and I don't think anyone of us ever thought we would be in California in 1967. I'm here, its 1966. I won't be here next year.

He stated, "That a change of cycle was coming about. He said the earth went through cycles of so many thousands of years and as one cycle closed out, the next one started." It wasn't any abrupt action like flipping a switch, now its day, now its night, but one ebbed out, the other came in. He said the coming of the new one had already started or was about to start at that time it seems, and that the new one would not be in full swing until around the year 2000."

He said, "That there would have to be many geographical changes made in preparation for this, there will have to be many changes in other systems." He said, "As a result of this, there would be many religious upheavals, political upheavals and so on, that will be of natural consequence, because the political leaders won't have the answers for these things. They can only answer so many things that happen, but beyond that, its a miracle or an act of God, but all of a sudden God is here."

He referred to Christ as Christ Jesus, and he said that, "He was a Son of God, but not the Son of God." In other words, "There were many, many millions of Sons of God of different degrees. He was just a higher degree of intelligence of a Son of God when he visited here." He said, "In this day and age he would be called nothing more than a clairvoyant being and that's all." He said that, "Most of your predictions of the miracles in the Bible are built up out of proportion." He said, "You can actually assimilate the realization of them if you were to, so to speak, gear them back down. That it is possible and they are happening around you every day. You just don't label them as a miracle and write them off the book."

He said, "Out of the entire thing, there would be much holocaust." He said, "At one time, it was possible for the civilization to save itself." He said, "The people of the earth produce vibrations, and these are positive and negative vibrations and there are vibrations of love and, as we know, there are many forms of love. He said that the vibrations were however, overwhelmingly so negative. The world was overwhelmingly materialistic and they were no longer objective to things which they could not see. They would rather have something they can hold on to." We will find out of course, ourselves, we don't possess anything, nothing, not even our children.

I think its how we use it as well as ourselves, we're sort of licensed to operate ourselves here. I'm not sure which department issues this license, but we have the use of the land, we have the use of the air, the use of the water, it would seem. There is no tax to be paid on this, except to the, shall we say, the Universal Law of Cause and Effect. And he went into some degree in this, explaining what we have come to know now as a Karmic pattern. This is an old law of the Far East.

During our communication, they made a statement pertaining to religion in which they stated, they said, "There are four major erroneous religious concepts on your planet at this time." They said, "These are Mohammedism, Buddhism, Brahma and Christianity." He said he defined reincarnation more specifically. He said, "They went through voluntarily, reincarnation." He said, "However, we are not quite at that level of consciousness here. That most people won't even accept it, let alone know how to utilize it or how to utilize their past lives."

He said, "Reincarnation is just as simple as grade school." He said, "You go to first grade; you study the subject matter, and at the end of the year you take the examination, and one of three things happen. Number one - you pass, and you go on to the next grade, the next higher step and higher opportunity. Number two - you fail the test, and you take the grade over." In other words, you come back; you get another vehicle, another body; you go through it again, second chance. "Number three - you fail the test or you fail earlier in the schedule and you drop out, and you drop out and you float around for hundreds, maybe thousands of years before coming into a state of awareness that you can come back and eventually come back."

"If you examine your child prodigies and the intellects of your different people, he said, you will find that number one, you will find many of the answers there." And he said, "You will also find that a child upon close investigation, until they are about three or four years old, has vivid recollections of their past lives." He said, "It won't take much investigation for you to find this out." "Study your own children, he said, many of the little stories they are telling aren't stories, it has already happened to them."

He went into diet. He said, "They were vegetarians. They do not consume meat because the animals contain spirit bodies just as we do; contain the spirit." He said, "We do not believe in destroying the vehicle of the spirit or altering their Karmic pattern." He said that, "They do not believe in inebriation." He did not say, we don't drink, he didn't say they didn't drink, he said, "They do not believe in intoxicating the body," that's how they worded it.

The predictions he stated at that time; they discussed Cuba. He said, "An island close to the southeast of the United States would be taken over by the 'Bear'. He said he always referred to them as the Great Bear, the Russians." And he said that, "A major conflict would arise out of a seemingly insignificant war or insignificant conflict in the southeastern part of Asia," which we might call Viet Nam. He said, "This would seemingly be very small and insignificant, but it would advance to the stage which could be a major war between the three major powers in which he said, the Great Bear would join with the Americans against the Orientals."

Now, remember back in 1954, about the biggest threat that China had on winning a war was throwing rice, and now they have nuclear power. This to me is not nearly the threat that germ warfare is. Its true, they still don't have an air force, they don't have a navy; they don't need it. All they need is a couple of submarines and get close enough and you got an epidemic. We can bring it in ourselves! We still import some things from China. We can import the entire death and destruction of this country. You know how big a germ is? People say, "What's a flu epidemic?" That's just as fast as it spreads, it goes pretty fast, doesn't it? Germ warfare can wipe out a nation just as fast; not sick, dead! You say, so what! You're coming back anyway!

The overture of this entire thing, the seeking and then the why, what to do, where do we go from here? He stated that, "This Master told him that out of the entire holocaust, 7,000,000 people would survive." Do you know what 7,000,000 is in the population of the planet? Its a drop in the bucket, very few! He said, "How will they survive?" He said, "They will be the ones who will find their own salvation." He said, "They will heed the warnings." He said, "What do you mean by warnings?"

Well, he had made a prediction. He stated that, "There would be a major land change in Southern California in 1967, he said, but there would be two warning signs. He said 90 days before this, the volcanoes of Mt. Pelee or Mt. Vesuvius would erupt." He said, When this happens, for those who heed it, he said, they will move; for those who don't, they will find Southern California inundated under the waters of the Pacific Ocean." He said, "These waters will extend as far inland and north as far as Salt Lake City, Utah." That's an awful lot of land, that's a lot of people. That takes care of seven million right there; I don't know how many more.

He said, "There would be major land changes, geographical changes all over the planet in preparation." It was of interest to me, I see a gentleman friend of mine seated in the back there, who showed me an article a few weeks ago, a little article which stated, relating how an island emerged out of the Pacific Ocean off the coast of Chile, witnessed by many people. Its still there, it didn't go back down, its still there; an island 60 miles long!

In some other predictions or prophecies that he made, it is stated that before the continent of Japan, the greater part of the Pacific Ocean will emerge from the Pacific. There will be the emergence of land mass in the southern Pacific. When an island comes up out of the Pacific, that's land mass.

There are many ways you can interpret or misinterpret many things. Its very difficult to be objective at times, to be realistic. And you say, first, we want the facts, then what do we do with them. He said, "Its too late for the planet as a whole." He said, "By the time your children are four or five years old they are so thoroughly indoctrinated to prejudice, hatred, distrust, selfishness, he said, you block the doors to them." He said, "There is your only hope." He said, "We begin to educate our children when they are three months old. By the time they are fifteen years of age, they have mastered telepathy."

The Colonel never did this, he never dictated to us. He never said at any time, this is so, this is the way it will be, this is what you have to do; he never said that. He said, "Here it is. Do what you want with it. Take it or leave it."

We were separated in 1957, and I went back to Connecticut, to my home state. And I had given him the address of my parents back there, and I went into business in Connecticut. And for two years I thought, awe, just bury it, just bury it, don't think about it. A number of little things happen and the subject comes up and you can't talk about it, so you don't, and you sit there and say, well gee, I wonder what it would be worth if they knew what I knew, if it would help them any. You say, well, I better not. So you just sit there and listen to them talk about it.

In 1959, September, my mother called me at the office. She said, "You got a telegram here from Colonel so and so." I said, "Well, open it, read it to me," so she did, and he was at the Westchester County Airport in White Plains, New York. There was a phone number there, and I called him. He says, "Come on down. Let's get together." He sounded very happy. So I did. I went right down and saw him, and he was very happy. He was probably the happiest man I had ever seen, and we went over old times for a few minutes.

And I said, "What's happening Pete?" He said, "I made it! I made the grade! I'm going on!" I said, "Oh, did you get a promotion?" And he said, "No, I'm going with them." And I said, "Boy", I said, "Its been awhile, let me sit down for this. What do you mean by going with them?" He says, "I'm going with them, just the way it sounds." And I said, "How much time do you have?" And he said, "About thirty days, within thirty days I'm going." Well, we talked about other things, and he came up to the house a couple of times.

If he wasn't at the base, I called the base every day from then on, twice a day, sometimes three times a day. Sometimes I called he wouldn't be there of course, so I would leave a message and he'd call me back. And its like waiting for a baby, except in reverse, you're waiting for someone to leave. You happy about it, you wonder! I told him, "You don't seem to be upset about this. You don't have any fear." He said, "No, I'm probably one of the happiest men you'll ever know." He said, "I'm looking forward to this like a kid to Christmas." He said, "I'm going and I know it!" He said, "Its a terrific feeling, let me tell you." He said, "But I know where I'm going, I guess that helps." I said, "Do you really, do you really know where you're going?" He said, "Wherever it is, its right, and whatever it is, I found it." And he said, "Let me tell you, you keep seeking and you'll find it." He said, "Just don't, don't ever misuse it. Don't ever misinterpret it. Always be objective, never dictate with it, and he said, you'll find the Truth."

On the twenty-seventh day I called down there and they told me he was out and they took a message to have him call me and he didn't call me back. So I called again, and they said, "No, he was overdue." He was on a mission, he was out over the Atlantic Ocean. And so I waited and called back, and they said, "No, he was reported missing, assumed down." And I said, "Well, have you launched a search?" And they said, "Yes". And I said, "Is it a major or minor search?" And they said, "Minor search." And I said, "How long to a major search?" And he said, "We can't tell you that."

Now a search is a very expensive proposition, man and materials. It may cost $40,000. to search for somebody just in a matter of hours, and they just don't call a major search right away. There is so many hours on a local search, minor search, and then they go into a major search. So I asked him how far the major search was off, and he told me so many minutes. This answered my question in another way, so I said, "Fine." So I called back in the morning, and he said, "No trace, presumed lost," and after so much time of course, the searching time is off; when its off, its finished. And I asked him if there was anything, and they said, "No, no trace." To my knowledge, they haven't, they haven't found him, never did.

This, of course, is nothing, nothing original about this. There are some 800 military personnel that disappear every year without report of where they are, where they went. This is in the air, I don't know how many disappear on the ground. I am now associated with a man who resigned his position in Washington just two months ago who was with this assignment. He was one of the heads of this. To sit and listen to the things that he tells, makes this mild. And he wants to get it out too, Its not easy. Its as I say, not to dictate, just to say, here it is, do with it what you want.

I understand we're going to have a question and answer series. I imagine some of you do have some questions. There are some questions I cannot answer, will not, but will be glad to if you have any.

Question:

Are other countries releasing the information concerning flying saucers to their people?

Answer:

As far as the information concerning the saucer is concerned, we find that the Netherlands, Sweden, and Brazil have come out and openly presented the information, the facts of the matter, the fact that they exist. I understand that its being taught in the schools in the Netherlands.

Question:

Pertaining to geographical changes in California, was all of California to be inundated?

Answer:

It seems as it was related to me, no, the southern portion. In other words, probably the lower half of the state. I am being very brief in this, because in order to be more specific, I would have to have a map here to outline the area of the Sierra Nevada Mountain Range, and some of the other mountain ranges along the fault, because there is a great valley here that would certainly go down. It would seem that the series of events will be an earthquake, and there will be a settling of land mass, and then it will be followed by a tidal wave and then the resurge or the tidal wave of the water will draw much of the land out. On one of these maps, you have a topography, I shouldn't say topography, that's an elevation, where you also have a depth gauge on here as to how this descends off the coastline, and we're on a shelf. You don't have to go out very far where the depth of it is 2,000 ft. It drops very, very fast which means that the shelf can drop, it just merely settles; it goes right down. This really describes the Pacific Palisades; the entire coast is just like that. In other words, the sides of a hill slides down.

Question:

Please be more specific about the signs when Pelee and or Vesuvius erupts?

Answer:

He did say and or Vesuvius or Pelee. He merely stated the eruption of these volcanoes, not a sign, but the eruption of these volcanoes, either one, and within 90 days it would happen.

Question:

What is the life span of space people?

Answer:

I don't know. It would seem from certain comments that he made, they control this more than anything. He mentioned that they go through voluntary reincarnation, through cell regeneration. In other words, they actually reduce themselves back to the atomic state in a matter of minutes. He said they can do this anytime. He said, "They usually do this in cycles of 50 years, because the younger body learns faster, and that they renew this cycle at that time." He did say that, "The average appearance of them was that when they were about 80 years of age, they appear to be in their late teens related to what we know."

Question:
Can you elaborate and or comment on the piece of wrapping paper incident as involved with a gun camera shot of one of the earlier X-15 flights at the giant object which it actually boarded?

The wrapping paper incident? I am not sure what exactly is meant by the wrapping paper incident. I am not familiar with that term. I am aware of some of the pictures taken by X-15's. I have seen pictures taken by the astronauts also.

Question:
Is it true that the government wants you to stop talking about UFO's? If so, why?

Answer:
From much, much, and I say much, enough information to fill a room which does not agree with the current political situation, or way of thinking of this government or any other governments, is one reason. Political imagery is a situation which you have to, in essence, put up the best front, no matter what the truth is. The government faces some bad situations, some very embarrassing, just as much as we become involved personally at times. The truth seems to hurt. We have to face up to it. They are running a race. Now, what this race is with, or where it is going to take them, would seem from all of this information, that they are going to exhaust and burn themselves out with it, and this is the only place it can take them. Now, as to whether you want to aid and abet that, I think there's coming to be a certain amount of awareness or consciousness on the part of many people, not just yourselves, as to what's right.

Why doesn't the government want me to talk about it? Because I represented the government. Its an inside story. Its not outside the door. Its not on the sidewalk. It came from inside the office. This is why. What length will they go to stop it? I don't know. I could write a book of my experiences with the F.B.I. so far. Only time will tell what that will bring.

Question:
I know a Colonel in UFO investigation about 1957, 58 or so who spoke in tongues. Is that your Colonel?

Answer:
I can't answer the question. I don't know.

Question:

Have you any knowledge of mass deportation of people by UFO's at the time of the catastrophe, the holocaust?

Answer:

There has been certain information he related himself. He stated, "That there would be certain numbers of people who would be deported, who would be removed safely." He said, "However, it doesn't make much difference if you're going to go, you're going to go, because he said, you just lose the vehicle, that's all, you still come back again."

He said, "Actually, what was spoken of as the Ark during the flood, was a mother-ship which was evacuating thousands of individuals." He said, "The bit about the two of each type of thing, he said, I don't know about that." He said that was just a mother-ship evacuating individuals during the time of the flood. He said, "The same thing won't happen again."

Question:

As is obvious, the space people want to help us, why doesn't our government go all out to accept this and inform the people accordingly?

Answer:

I think we more or less covered this before. To put it mildly, the government has got the tiger by the tail with this thing. It is leaking out. Secret. Top Secret. Confidential. Security. Anything stamped with that. We used to have a stamp in operations at the field. It said, "TOP SECRET: DESTROY BEFORE READING." Its leaking out.

Question:

Are they like angels?

Answer:

I think there are many descriptions for angels.

Question:

Where does angels leave spiritual and become mortal?

Answer:

I think these people certainly have the answers. I think that they are, possibly can even, they can control the change almost at will it would seem. Not having seen them, I've never seen them so I don't know.

Question:

Have you received any messages by means of ESP or otherwise with the lost Colonel?

Answer:

The fields related to this subject are almost unlimited. They go into the political realms, the realms of medicine, of religions, spirituality, psychic, occult, even the drug market. In essence, what they represent at times, is a thousand cliffs to dive off. Take any one of them, and you can interpret a great deal of what they have to fit. Many people have come to me, they came to me in the past, and they said, "How would you like to speak to the Colonel?" I said, "Swell," and they said, "We can do it, set it up for you, have a little meeting." And I attended some number of these, and basically, they are one form or another of the spiritual seance. Some used different vehicles and tools; others didn't. And before each one of these, I would ask them, "You know, to tell you the truth, I don't know where the other two pilots are, and , and I would just as soon know their address, their location at this time, because its very important to me." And I said, "If you can produce this for me, I will be just as happy with your authenticity as if you had produced the Colonel, and in truth, I would be more pleased."

Well, they produced many voices; they produced many other things, but they never produced the addresses of these two other pilots, and I found them just by accident the day after Thanksgiving last year where I have located them after eight years.

With the exception of one individual, and this woman shook me up real good just a few weeks ago. I'm not too, pardon the expression, hep on these things, on people who can give you a reading; I'm not even familiar with the hows, the mechanics behind it. I'm no detector, I don't know how to tell the real one from the bad one, unless I have some results.

This woman pinned me from day one, right through the future. She came up with a thousand things, spoke of places, times, incidents, people that I had known and done things with. When it came to the Colonel, I asked her what she could tell me about a man named Colonel Peterson. Now, she was totally unaware of who I was or what my experiences had been before this. She thought for a minute and her first question to me was, "Do you know how he died?" She didn't know he was dead. I said, "No." She said, "Do you know if they ever found the body?" And I said, "No." She said, "He didn't die in the regular way that we know it." She said, "Its funny, she said, he's still in his physical form. He wants to talk to you very badly!" She said, "He's been trying to reach you for a long time." She said, "You're going to be talking to him within a year." She said, "But there will be two men come to see you before that to prepare you." Well, she had already told me all these several hundred things, about things that I had done, people I knew, and things that I had done, funny things, embarrassing things. I don't know; the odds are phenomenal. She really struck it home. Time will tell. She made a number of other predictions.

To my knowledge, I have not corresponded with him in any way, shape or form. I am unaware of it if I have. Perhaps he can read my mind now; I don't know.

Question:
        Could these UFO's be our own experiments, and is the Air Force evaluating public reaction on observations and how our different possible explanations on these things they would see?

Answer:
        At this time there are a number of aircraft corporations; Hughes, Bell, North American and some eastern firms who are on heavy government contracts on anti-gravity. This is the assignment; find the way to control gravity. I understand MIT has developed a system, a propulsion unit, to control a small model instrument package with the same means of control. I understand that it could not develop it. The weight of it is too much to lift a payload, in other words, to put a man in it. However, they are working on this system.

As to how any other system, jet, internal combustion, steam, nuclear, any other form of propulsion, could accomplish the things that we saw, I don't think it could be done. We have developed a saucer appearing aircraft, but they are notably slow and cumbersome. They are mostly in the verticle take-off type of field.

Question:

The Bahai faith has many parallels to those predictions you have just covered. Is this faith one of the true religions mentioned?

Answer:

It would seem, many people say, they'll compare with my remarks, relations to many religions. They will say, "Are you Mormon? Are you Mohammedan? Are you Buddhist? Are you this or that?" My answer to them is that I am a roving Christian. I accept, I believe God, but I do not follow any particular concept of it. Their statement also to us was, "That there are many original truths in all of these religions, but they are so varied and misconceived and misinterpreted that it would be a lifetime alone just trying to sift it out, and this is the problem, sifting, this constant sifting, trying to find the truth out of it." I am not well worded or that familiar with the Bahai faith to draw the parallels myself, so I don't know. It may be very true.

Question:

You stated you wouldn't be in California in 1967. Question; Where will you be?

Answer:

I don't know. I haven't decided it at this time. It will be a high elevation, I guarantee you that.

Question:

What area of direction would you head or what country?

Answer:

Once again I refer to this basic elevation of 4,000 ft. or over. It seems that this is the best.

Question:

Do you know of a spacecraft reportedly at Edwards Air Force Base? I have heard that it is under guard in a large hanger.

Answer:

I have talked with military who have stated that there have been, not one, but several saucers at Edwards Air Force Base. Actually, there's a lot of talk about Edwards Air Force Base out here, because its in California. The actual base which is designated for all this type of thing, for all of the evidence, physical evidence pertaining to saucers, is at Wright Patterson Air Force Base at Dayton, Ohio. That's Air Material Command. This is where they take everything and put the 'Top Secret' on it, and from things that I have heard, they have really got quite a museum there. I haven't been there. I don't think I have a ticket to the gate when I get there. Especially me!

Question:

You said the Christian religion was wrong. Which religion is right?

Answer:

No, I did not say that the Christian religion was wrong. It would seem that the, once again, that these religions, all of them, contain the original truths, or Universal Laws as such, but they are not correctly interpreted. They have gotten materialistic. They have changed their objectives to other things which are easier.

I was reading an article the other day by an Indian, a Hindu. He said, "You know, church, the objective of church is merely to make people think happy, just to make them think they're secure. Don't give them the truth, because they don't want it. It just scares the daylights out of them and what good is that going to do? Who wants to go around scaring people? A successful church is the one that makes the most people feel at ease. This is the one that can give them a way of life to go by, that's the easiest rolling wheel chair." That's what it amounts to and there are many churches that do this of course. Now that church, that doesn't mean that that church was found on those principals, that they have always preached those things. We have seen radical changes in the last few years in a number of the churches, the beliefs, of this earth. We see a breaking up of the old and the new, the moderates they call it. I heard a lecture delivered a few months ago by a man who was defining a square, exactly what a square is. By all his definitions, it pays off to be a square. It probably does.

Question:

You mentioned that your radar vectored you to a target not available by the human eye, not visible to be photographed by infra-red film.

Answer:

No, I did not say that we were vectored by radar. We were not. To my knowledge, we had no control from ground control, no directions from ground control. It was possible, I said, to be vectored by radar on a target and to shoot it with infra-red film and to produce a picture you could not see. We were not, though.

Question:

Any other means of power guidance in flight?

Answer:

I assume this pertains to a saucer. There are many theories on this by the way. I don't know exactly what the answer to it is. It would seem there are many theories, some make more sense than others. Its not inconceivable that they could use several means, any one of several means to do it. I've heard of the solar energy theory as well as the local electrical field energy theory, gas theory, nuclear theories.

Question:

Are you able to give out any other geographical changes coming to Earth as foretold by the Master?

Answer:

This pertained mostly to Europe and to Japan. He stated that, "In '67, that the same fault line that would open here, runs through the Pacific Ocean and up through Japan, and that it would take the greater part of Japan with it.

Question:

You said that there were spacecraft guarded at these varies Air Force Bases, or these so-called flying saucers. You said something about these spacecraft being locked up under tight security regulations?

Answer:

This is what information I have.

Question:

How did they acquire possession of such spacecraft or aircrafts?

Answer:

I understand that they were delivered voluntarily, all but one exception. It seems one crashed and it was captured that way; it was recovered, the wreckage was recovered.

Question:

Is it a fact that these flying saucers are from outer space and that they have an accident and are recovered?

Answer:

They're not perfect either it seems. They malfunction also.

Question:

What's your opinion of the temperature inside the Earth?

Answer:

Not having been there, I don't know.

Question:

What about the hollow Earth theory?

Answer:

There's an awful lot of information pertaining to this hollow Earth theory. If you take two people and say, here, you take a pro and you take a con, we can build quite a case on either side, for and against it. My opinion, I'm neutral. I'm right down the middle at this point. I've investigated it as to the source, I mean, as far as I can go to the source. There must be much more as far as the sources pertain, but I'll keep going to find the answer about that. Right now, I'm in the middle of the road.

Question:

Going back to your comment on the belt and disk held in the hand. You said disk?

Answer:

Disk, round, oval; that's right.

Question:

Not a jewel, but a disk?

Answer:

No, a disk. It looked like a miniature saucer. It wasn't a scale model as such, it was completely polished disk, and he submitted this to a metalurgic laboratory for examination. Their report was most interesting but of course, they wanted to know where he got it.

Question:

Has he still got the disk, that thing that he had?

Answer:

I don't know what he did with that. He's gone, so I don't know.

Question:

Have the astronauts seen flying saucers?

Answer:

I understand, yes. I've seen some photographs allegedly taken by Scott Carpenter. They were fairly close-up. I don't know how these could have been duped, because they were taken from the window of the capsule and you could see the earth below, similar to the pictures that you would see in Life Magazine. In other words, the distance and the position of the capsule in relation to the earth's surface, but the saucers were right there, right outside!

Question:

I have talked to Scott Carpenter myself, and I have secret clearance and of course, I have to be careful in what I say because I work for the government. But Scott Carpenter told me that at no time when any of the astronauts are up there that they are alone. They are under constant surveillance by these people at all times. The question I want to ask is this. I too am aware by direct contact from the Brothers, that they have craft at Edwards Air Force Base. Now the question in mind is this; These craft are there for the United States government to study and obviously they know how to control them, then why all of the different contracts to discover and find out why and what makes them operate? I believe they already have the answer or should have because they have these craft to study.

Answer:

From what information I have received, is that we are not capable of operating them, that we can study them. We are attempting to assimulate from the information received from the study to construct, to evolve to that point. However, to my knowledge, we have not been able to operate one at this point. I've had information for some odd years to the effect that Canada has had two of them which they obtained as gifts. They have these in concrete bunkers in the inland and they've studied these for years but they haven't come up with the answers yet.

Question:

Did the UFO's have anything to do with the blackout in New York?

Answer:

This may interest some others beside you. I'm having an interview tomorrow evening with a gentleman who was in New York City during the blackout, who states that he had a contact and saw saucers there and was told by this contact. Now, this man, I won't say his name, this man is a very big figure.

Question:

Is he the man who was in a newspaper clipping? Was he an actor?

Answer:

Yes. He's a well known actor. I'm only going to compare what he's going to tell me, that's all.

Question:

Do you think the Colonel was taken aboard another craft and that's where he is now?

Answer:

My opinion, yes.

Question:

You mean he was actually taken to another planet?

Answer:

That's my opinion, sir. I don't know. I haven't been there to see him yet.

Question:

What was the purpose of the blackout if the UFO's engineered it?

Answer:

Merely a demonstration. That's once again, my opinion; I don't know.

Question:

What would life be like inside this planet and other planets of this system?

Answer:

Once again, I haven't been there. I don't know how to answer that, unless you can find somebody that's been there. We've been so wrong, so wrong, totally wrong, about the moon, space, other planets, from what little we have seen, what little we've brought back, what little we've sent back, its reversed the theories and the way of thinking of scientists, nuclear physicists, mathematicians, all these years. And these men are going around shaking their heads now.

I was talking to a nuclear physicists who works at Vandenberg Air Force Base a couple of months ago, and he said, "You know, if we've reversed a dozen, we've reversed at least 5,000 theories in the last few years." This is how fast they're changing now with what they're finding out there, and much of it is just the opposite of what they thought before.

Question:

Just recently I read a book by Dino Kraspedon. The name of the book is "My Contact with Flying Saucers". That book I think fits the nearest description on this I've ever read. I've read thirty or forty different books on this story. I believe that anyone that would read that would get a lot of questions answered. It deals with the vacuum that these flying saucers travel in. They create their own vacuum.

Answer:

He talked about this vacuum, created with a ray. He described this to us. This is above my mathematics and chemistry. I can't get up that far but he explained it fairly well for us to understand. This eliminates, of course, the gravity, yaw and lift.

Question:

What happens to the photographs of UFO's?

Answer: If there are photographs, if you can get them to somebody else, before the FBI gets to you, then there's a chance they'll get out. If they get to you first, as far as government photos are concerned, the only way they're going to get out is from somebody from the inside getting them out. We saw hundreds and hundreds of photographs and hours of motion picture films taken from jets and gun cameras, but that film has never been released, never been released and won't be. Thank you.